D1428243

# STIRRINGS STILL

# STIRRINGS STILL

Samuel Beckett

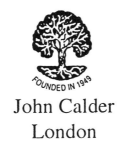

John Calder
London

First published in this edition by
John Calder Publishers 1999
London

*Stirrings Still* first published by John Calder (Publishers) Ltd in a
deluxe edition illustrated by Louis Le Brocquy, limited to 200
copies and signed by author and artist in 1988. Subsequently
republished in *As The Story Was Told* 1990. *What Is the Word*
first published in English in *As The Story Was Told* 1990 and by
Editions de minuit in French 1990.

ISBN 0 7145 43047
Paperback


British Library Cataloguing in Publication Data
A catalogue record for this title is available from the British
Library

Printed in Canada by Webcom Ltd

# STIRRINGS STILL

# STIRRINGS STILL

## I

One night as he sat at his table head
on hands he saw himself rise and go.
One night  or day. For when his own
light went out he was not left in the
dark. Light of a kind came then from
the one high window. Under it still
the stool on which till he could or
would no more he used to mount to

see the sky. Why he did not crane out to see what lay beneath was perhaps because the window was not made to open or because he could or would not open it. Perhaps he knew only too well what lay beneath and did not wish to see it again. So he would simply stand there high above the earth and see through the clouded pane the cloudless sky. Its faint unchanging light unlike any light he could remember from the days and nights when day followed hard on night and night on day. This outer light then when his own went out became his only light till it in its turn went out and left him in the dark. Till it in its turn went out.

One night or day then as he sat at his table head on hands he saw himself rise and go. First rise and stand clinging to the table. Then sit again. Then rise again and stand clinging to the table again. Then go. Start to go. On unseen feet start to go. So slow that only change of place to show he went. As when he disappeared only to reappear later at another place. Then disappeared again only to reappear again later at another place again. So again and again disappeared again only to reappear again at another place again. Another place in the place where he sat at his table head on hands. The same place and table as when Darly for example died and left him. As when others too in their turn before and since. As when others would too in their turn and leave him till he too in his turn. Head on hands half hoping when he disappeared again that he would not reappear again and half fearing that he would not. Or merely wondering. Or merely waiting. Waiting to see if he would or would not. Leave him or not alone again waiting for nothing again.

Seen always from behind whithersoever he went. Same hat and coat as of old when he walked the roads. The back roads. Now as one in a strange place seeking the way out. In the dark. In a strange place blindly in the dark of night or day seeking the way out. A way out. To the roads. The back roads.

A clock afar struck the hours and half-hours. The same as when among others Darly once died and left him. Strokes now clear as if carried by a wind now faint on the still air. Cries afar now faint now clear. Head on hands half hoping when the hour struck that the half-hour would not and half fearing that it would not. Similarly when the half-hour struck. Similarly when the cries a moment ceased. Or merely wondering. Or merely waiting. Waiting to hear .

There had been a time he would sometimes lift his head enough to see his hands. What of them was to be seen. One laid on the table and the other on the one. At rest after all they did. Lift his past head a moment to see his past hands. They lay it back on them to rest it too. After all it did.

The same place as when left day after day for the roads. The back roads. Returned to night after night. Paced from the wall to wall in the dark. The then fleeting dark of night. Now as if strange to him seen to rise and go. Disappear and reappear at another place. Disappear again and reappear again at another place again. Or at the same. Nothing to show not the same. No wall toward which or from. No table back toward which or further from. In the same place as when paced from wall to wall all places as the same. Or in another. Nothing to show not another. Where never. Rise and go in the same place as ever. Disappear and reappear in another where never. Nothing to show not another where never. Nothing but the strokes. The cries. The same as ever.

Till so many strokes and cries since he was last seen that perhaps he would not be seen again. Then so many cries since the strokes were last heard that perhaps they would not be heard again. Then such silence since the cries were last heard that perhaps even they would not be heard again.

Perhaps thus the end. Unless no more than a mere lull. Then all as before. The strokes and cries as before and he as before now there now gone now there again now gone again. Then the lull again. Then all as before again. So again and again. And patience till the one true end to time and grief and self and second self his own.

## 2

As one in his right mind when at last out again he knew not how he was not long out again when he began to wonder if he was in his right mind. For could one not in his right mind be reasonably said to wonder if he was in his right mind and bring what is more his remains of reason to bear on this perplexity in the way he must be said to do if he is to be said at all? It was therefore in the guise of a more or less reasonable being that he emerged at last he knew not how into the outer world and had not been there for more than six or seven hours by the clock when he could not but begin to wonder if he was in his right mind. By the same clock whose strokes were those heard times without number in his confinement as it struck the hours and half hours and so in a sense at first a source of reassurance till finally one of alarm as being no clearer now than when in principle muffled by his four walls. Then he sought help in the thought of one hastening westward at sundown to obtain a better view of Venus and found it of none. Of the sole other sound that of cries enlivener of his solitude as lost to suffering he sat at his table head on hands the same was true. Of their whenceabouts that is of clock and cries the same was true that is no more to be determined now than as was only natural then. Bringing to bear on all this his remains of reason he sought help in the thought that his memory of indoors was perhaps at fault and found it of none. Further to his disarray his soundless tread as when barefoot he trod his floor. So all ears from bad to worse till in the end he ceased if not to hear to listen and set out to look about him. Result finally he was in a  field of grass which went some way if nothing else to explain his tread and then a little later as if to make up for this some way to increase his trouble. For he could recall no field of grass from even the very heart of which no limit of any kind was to be discovered but always in some quarter or another some end in sight such as a fence or other manner of bourne from which to return. Nor on his looking more closely to make matters worse was this the short green grass he seemed to remember eaten down by flocks and herds but long and light grey in colour verging here and there on white. Then he sought help in the thought that his memory of outdoors was perhaps at fault and found it of none. So all eyes from bad to worse till in the end he ceased if not to look (about him or more closely) and set out to take thought. To this end for want of a stone on which to sit like Walther and cross his legs the best he could do was stop dead and stand stock still which after a moment of hesitation he did and of course sink his head as one deep in meditation which after another moment of hesitation he did also. But soon weary of vainly delving in those remains he moved on through the long hoar grass resigned to not knowing where he was or how he got there or where he was going or how to get back to whence he knew not how he came. So on unknowing and no end in sight. Unknowing and what is more no wish to know nor indeed any wish of any kind nor therefore any sorrow save that he would have wished the strokes to cease and the cries for good and was sorry that they did not. The strokes now faint now clear as if carried by the wind  but not a breath and the cries now faint now clear.

# 3

So on till stayed when to his ears from deep within oh how and here a word he could not catch it were to end where never till then. Rest then before again from not long to so long that perhaps never again and then again faint from deep within oh how and here that missing word again it were to end where never till then. In any case whatever it might be to end and so on was he not already as he stood there all bowed down and to his ears faint from deep within again and again oh how something and so on was he not so far as he could see already there where never till then?

For how could even such a one as he
having once found himself in such a
place not shudder to find himself in it
again which he had not done nor
having shuddered seek help in vain in
the thought so-called that having
somehow got out of it then he could
somehow get out of it again which he
had not  done either. There then all
this time where never till then and so
far as he could see in every direction
when he raised his head and opened
his eyes no danger or hope as the case
might be of his ever getting out of it.
Was he then now to press on regard-
less now in one direction and now in
another or on the other hand stir no
more as the case might be  that is as

that missing word might be which if to warn such as sad or bad for example then of course in spite of all the one and if the reverse then of course the other that is stir no more. Such and much more such the hubbub in his mind so-called till nothing left from deep within but only ever fainter oh to end. No matter how no matter where. Time and grief and self so-called. Oh all to end.

for Barney Rosset

# WHAT IS THE WORD

# WHAT IS THE WORD

folly -
folly for to -
for to -
what is the word -
folly from this -
all this -
folly from all this -
given -
folly given all this -
seeing -

folly seeing all this -
this -
what is the word -
this this -
this this here -
all this this here -
folly given all this -
seeing -
folly seeing all this this here -
for to -
what is the word -
see -
glimpse -
seem to glimpse -
need to seem to glimpse -
folly for to need to seem to glimpse -
what -
what is the word -

and where -
folly for to need to seem to glimpse
                          what where -
where -
what is the word -
there -
over there -
away over there -
afar -
afar away over there -
afaint -
afaint afar away over there what -
what -
what is the word -
seeing all this -
all this this -
all this this here -
folly for to see what -

glimpse -
seem to glimpse -
need to seem to glimpse -
afaint afar away over there what -
folly for to need to seem to glimpse
  afaint afar away over there what -
what -
what is the word -

what is the word